For Hattie

First published 1990 by Walker Books Ltd
87 Vauxhall Walk, London SE11 5HJ

This edition published 1991

© 1990 Margaret Gordon

Printed and bound in Hong Kong by
Sheck Wah Tong Printing Press Ltd

British Library Cataloguing in Publication Data
Gordon, Margaret
Getting to know Cousin Rodney.
I. Title
823'.914 [J]   PZ7
ISBN 0-7445-2008-8

Getting to Know
COUSIN RODNEY

Margaret Gordon

WALKER BOOKS
LONDON

One afternoon Mum agreed to look after
Cousin Rodney while Aunty Rosie went
to the hairdresser's.

Mum didn't know what to do with us, and she didn't know what to do with Cousin Rodney, so she took us all to the swings.

At the swings we found out lots of things
about Cousin Rodney that we hadn't
known before. We found out he was wild.
He didn't look wild.

We didn't know how clever he was.
He didn't look very clever.

We didn't know how heavy Cousin
Rodney was. He didn't look very heavy.

When the lady at the swings asked us to
leave, we ran about outside for a bit. . .

. . .until we were asked to leave there
as well.

Then we took Cousin Rodney home for tea.
Mum tried to make tea-time a little bit
special as Cousin Rodney was visiting.

We didn't know what sugar did to fizzy
lemonade. . .

or all the different things you can do with squashy cakes. . .

and jelly, until Cousin Rodney showed us.
We didn't know how hungry he was either.
He didn't look very hungry.

By the time Aunty Rosie came back from the hairdresser's, Mum looked like she knew all she wanted to know about Cousin Rodney. Aunty Rosie looked wonderful.

Then Aunty Rosie took Cousin Rodney home. We could tell he'd had a good time.

Until she got to know Cousin Rodney
better, Mum thought we were bad.
But now she says we're WONDERFUL!

MORE WALKER PAPERBACKS
For You to Enjoy

THE ADVENTURES OF OLD MOTHER HUBBARD'S DOG
by John Yeoman/Quentin Blake

Old Mother Hubbard is driven to distraction by the antics of her mischievous dog,
who takes up sport, dresses up, learns to play and needs a doctor in
these four verse adventures.
"Witty business as usual… This clever enterprise could go on for ever."
The Times Educational Supplement
ISBN 0-7445-2003-7 £4.50

AMY SAID
by Martin Waddell/Charlotte Voake

Staying at Gran's is a riot for Amy and her brother!
"A triumph… Understatement and lightness of touch couldn't find better exposition."
John Lawrence, The Times Educational Supplement
ISBN 0-7445-1779-6 £2.99

HAS ANYONE HERE SEEN WILLIAM?
by Bob Graham

What a merry dance young William leads his family!
He's never where he's supposed to be and always doing something he shouldn't!
"A fun book – lots of amusement but shown in a sympathetic way."
Signal Selection of Children's Books 1988
ISBN 0-7445-1339-1 £2.99

**Walker Paperbacks are available from most booksellers, or by post from
Walker Books Ltd, PO Box 11, Falmouth, Cornwall TR10 9EN.**

To order, send:
Title, author, ISBN number and price for each book ordered
Your full name and address
Cheque or postal order for the total amount, plus postage and packing:

UK, BFPO and Eire – 50p for first book, plus 10p for
each additional book to a maximum charge of £2.00.
Overseas Customers – £1.25 for first book,
plus 25p per copy for each additional book.
Prices are correct at time of going to press, but are subject to change without notice.